THE PRECIOUS RING

Lily
the Elf

Kane Miller
A DIVISION OF EDC PUBLISHING

For Sophie Liela Watts, who is an absolute delight. AB

For Es and all the little ones in my life. LC

Kane Miller, A Division of EDC Publishing

Text © Anna Branford 2015
Illustrations © 2015 Lisa Coutts
Cover and internal design copyright © Walker Books Australia

For information contact:
Kane Miller, A Division of EDC Publishing
PO Box 470663
Tulsa, OK 74147-0663
www.kanemiller.com
www.edcpub.com
www.usbornebooksandmore.com

Library of Congress Control Number: 2015957639
Printed and bound in the United States of America
1 2 3 4 5 6 7 8 9 10
ISBN: 978-1-61067-530-7

THE PRECIOUS RING

Lily
the Elf

Anna Branford

Illustrated by Lisa Coutts

Chapter one

Lily lives with her dad in a tiny elf house, hidden under a bridge in a busy city.

In the moss garden behind the house there is an even tinier house called a granny flat. And in the granny flat lives Lily's granny.

This morning, Dad is
going to help a friend
fix a broken toadstool.
As Lily waves good-bye,
she notices something
unusual in the garden.

It looks like a golden
hoop with jewels on one
side. The jewels make
rainbows all over the
garden.

It rained all night so
the hoop is full of water.
It makes a wading
pool fit for an elf princess,
Lily thinks. She jumps
in with a splash.

"What's all that splashing?" asks Granny, coming outside.

"It's my wading pool!" says Lily. "It was here when I woke up!"

Granny looks carefully.

"This is something special," says Granny. "It's a ring for a human finger."

Lily looks at her own fingers. "Humans are *huge*," she says.

"This one is for a small human," says Granny. "Maybe even a child."

"Is it precious?" asks Lily.

"I don't think so," says Granny. "It looks like painted plastic and glass."

"Hooray!" cheers Lily.
"Can we keep it then?"

She knows elves should
always return precious
lost things to the humans.

"I'm not sure," says
Granny. "Let's think
about it."

Lily does not need to think about it. She has already decided. She would like to keep the ring.

Chapter two

Lily splashes all morning,
while Granny knits.

They have lunch beside
the ring, watching their

funny reflections in the
curved gold.

In the afternoon,
Lily polishes the glass
jewels with a soft cloth.
The rainbows are even
brighter then.

"Look," says Lily.
"One of the jewels is
missing!"

"So it is," says Granny,
coming around to look.

"I think I know how we can fix that," says Granny. "We need some colored foil. The kind the humans wrap chocolates in. I'm sure I have some somewhere."

Lily wonders how chocolate wrappers will help. Before she can ask, they hear two human voices on the bridge. One voice is grown-up. The other is little.

"I dropped it down there," comes the little voice, sniffling.

"I'm afraid it's lost forever then," says the grown-up.

There is much more sniffling.

"It was only a plastic toy one," the grown-up says. "We'll get you another."

"But I loved *that* one." The human girl sounds about Lily's age. Lily has

lost a few things before.
She knows how it feels.

"Maybe she wasn't talking about the ring," says Lily. "She might have lost something different."

"Maybe," agrees Granny. "But it was something special. She sounded so sad. And the ring would be about the right size for her."

Lily thinks. The ring is about the right size for *her*. She would really like to keep her wading pool.

Chapter three

"Granny," says Lily, to change the subject, "how do you fix a missing jewel with a chocolate wrapper?"

Granny goes into her house and finds an old suitcase. It is full of huge pieces of colored foil.

Lily chooses a purple piece.

"The trick," Granny says, "is to scrunch it up."

Lily and Granny scrunch and scrunch together. Soon they have a big, sparkly purple ball.

"Now we need some glue," says Granny. She finds a tin of sticky tree sap. Granny paints the

gap in the ring with sap.
Then they press the foil
ball into it.

Soon the foil ball is
stuck in place.

The purple jewel
doesn't quite match the
others. But the ring looks
even more beautiful
than before.

By now the water is
warm from the sun on
the moss garden.

Lily doesn't feel like splashing. She lies in her wading pool and thinks.

Dad will be home soon. She can ask him about keeping the ring.

Maybe he will say, "I don't think you need to return it. It isn't the precious kind."

But Lily suspects that even plastic things can be precious, if someone really loves them.

After all, *she*
thinks the
ring is precious.
And she only
found it this
morning.

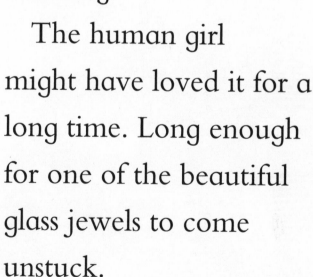

The human girl
might have loved it for a
long time. Long enough
for one of the beautiful
glass jewels to come
unstuck.

Lily has one last splash. Then she makes a decision.

Chapter four

When Dad gets home,
Lily shows him the ring.
"It's a real beauty,"
says Dad. "And what a

good wading pool."

"Good enough for an elf princess," says Lily softly. "I really wish I could keep it. But I think I want to give it back to the human who lost it."

"I think that's a good idea too," agrees Dad.

He helps Lily to lift up the side of the ring. The water drains out onto

the moss garden. Then
Lily uses an old towel to
dry and polish the gold
and jewels. Soon it is
sparkling like new.

Dad finds a long piece of thread in the shed. They tie one end tightly around the ring. Dad holds the other end and aims carefully. Then he throws it high up in the air. It loops over the railing of the bridge and tumbles back down.

Dad, Lily and Granny
all take hold of the
thread.

"One, two, THREE!"
yells Dad. They all pull
as hard as they can.

Soon the ring is
standing on its side.

"One, two, THREE!" yells Dad again. The ring dangles from the thread in midair.

They pull and pull
and the ring rises higher
and higher. Then there
is a little clink. The ring
has landed safely on the
bridge railing.

All evening long, Lily keeps looking up. She can still see the jewels sparkling on the bridge.

Chapter five

In the morning, Dad goes out early again. He is going to do more work on the broken toadstool.

Lily and Granny have
their breakfast together
in the moss garden. They
listen very carefully in
case the humans return.

After a while, they hear the sound of footsteps. Then suddenly there comes an excited sort of squeal.

"Mom! It's my ring!"

"It can't be," says the grown-up human. "We were right here just yesterday looking for it."

"But it is," says the little one, "it really is,

and it's sparklier!" Then
there is an even more
excited squeal. "Mom,
look! The missing jewel
has been fixed! There's
a purple one now."

Lily and Granny smile at each other.

"Amazing," says the grown-up. "I've never seen anything like it."

"There's a piece of thread tied to it!" says the small human as they walk over the rest of the bridge.

"I wonder who could have done that?"

But Lily and Granny don't hear the reply.

The moss garden is extra green and boggy where the wading pool was. And it is still good for splashing.

Other
Lily the Elf
books by
Anna Branford

The midnight owl
sounds scary!

Dandelion seed wishes
always come true –
don't they?

Lily the elf has a
brand-new elf flute.